RINEHART LIFTS

Other Avon Books by
R. R. Knudson

FOX RUNNING

R.R. KNUDSON grew up in Arlington, Virginia, which is also the home of Arthur Rinehart. She is the author of many sports novels for young readers and is herself a versatile athlete, as well as a writer, a reader, a former teacher, and a bird watcher. She lives in Sea Cliff, New York where she is currently working on two new books about boxing and weight lifting for kids. The author says, "Each of my books contains a lifting scene. I believe that people of every age help each other, lift each other, at crucial points in their lives—and that this deserves notice more than the let-downs of most young adult novels."

RINEHART LIFTS

R. R. KNUDSON

AN AVON CAMELOT BOOK

AVON BOOKS
A division of
The Hearst Corporation
959 Eighth Avenue
New York, New York 10019

First Camelot Printing, January, 1982

The Farrar, Straus & Giroux edition contains the following Library
of Congress Cataloging in Publication Data:

Library of Congress Cataloging in Publication Data

Knudson, R   Rozanne, 1932-
  Rinehart lifts.

  SUMMARY: Disappointed that her best friend is the
worst athlete in the fifth grade, Zan Hagen interests
Arthur Rinehart in lifting weights.
  [1. Weight lifting—Fiction. 2. Friendship—Fic-
tion] I. Title.
PZ7.K785.Ri   1980   [Fic]

In loving memory of my niece Ruth Meredith,
who has lifted us all

RINEHART LIFTS

Mr. Nobody   1

Zan Hagen bent over to pull her best friend, Rinehart, up from the dust. He'd fallen down chasing a soccer ball Zan had nudged past him.

"Rinehart, take my hand. Now—umph."

Up came Rinehart, smiling. No matter how many times he tripped he never got mad. He smiled when he stumbled into fences trying to stop the soccer ball. Smiling, he missed instead of kicked. He couldn't score, not one goal. He smiled at his zeros.

"Poor Rinehart," Zan said. She brushed off his woolly jacket. Puffs of dust made Rinehart sneeze. After that he fixed his glasses on straight. "Are you okay?" Zan asked, looking him over.

3

Poor Rinehart! He was not okay on field. He just wasn't athletic. You could notice that from any distance you saw him. Up close he had this sweet expression of Mr. Nice Guy. He couldn't look tough. Kids playing against him knew Rinehart would move out of their way.

And who was Rinehart anyway, on field? He seemed like Mr. Nobody. He didn't wear soccer shoes with plastic cleats. He wore his regular school shoes. He didn't own a striped shirt with big white numbers. He wore his school shirt under a heavy checkered jacket. That jacket kept Rinehart from being scraped when he fell down.

Rinehart fell down a lot. At a distance he looked like a tipping-over clown. He stabbed at the ball. Missed it. Rolled forward, until Zan hurried to help. Once on his feet again, Rinehart gave out with a cheer for Zan. Next he clapped for the other team. He couldn't learn to cheer the right guys. He moved up and down the field calling "Lovely kick" to his teammates, "Lovely kick" to the other team. He patted Zan on her back when she scored a goal. Same with every player.

"Don't cheer your enemies," Zan told Rinehart. "And don't hug them, whatever you do."

"Why not?" Rinehart asked.

"Pats and hugs help them kick better. I understand, because if you pat me I boom the ball miles. And when you hug me I score."

"I know that." Rinehart smiled his usual smile and shouted "Waytogo" at every soccer player. He waved his earmuffs.

Right around then, Zan Hagen felt like giving up on her pal. She had tried and tried to turn him into

4

an athlete. She couldn't begin to count all the balls she'd patiently thrown him. He always dropped them.

"Is this football too round?" Zan asked when he fumbled it.

"Is this too hard for you?" Zan asked about a softball.

"Too small?"

Rinehart lost a basketball tossed gently into his arms. "I tried," he explained.

"Rinehart, you couldn't catch the Goodyear blimp if it landed on your chest."

He couldn't throw, either. If he did, his hand went crooked. His wrist bumped his glasses.

"Is it too heavy?" Zan asked when he couldn't toss a Ping-Pong ball.

Rinehart smiled for an answer.

"Then roll it!" Zan pleaded.

Rinehart couldn't roll or toss or pitch or fling or bowl. He was uncoordinated as maple syrup. He was the slowest runner in fifth grade. Face it. Rinehart was a sports slouch.

But he didn't seem to care. He kept on coming to Zan's games. He waited around to be chosen for some team, any old team. He waited until last and never complained. What did he care?

Zan cared, of course. She sometimes felt sad having such a slouchy kid for best friend. When she wasn't trying to teach Rinehart sports, she was trying to figure out why she even liked him. She asked herself why she didn't like Randy Boyle best—Randy, the star. He could slam a soccer ball to China. His team called him the Hit Man. At after-school games Randy hit players and knocked them down. His team won by big scores because Randy was the star athlete

5

in Arlington County. Why shouldn't Zan make best friends with the Hit Man?

The Hit Man never chose Rinehart for his team. In fact, he usually wouldn't let Rinehart play at all. He took up a collection of pennies from every kid except Zan. He offered Rinehart twenty cents if he'd stay off field and not mess up either team.

"Make it a quarter," Rinehart said.

When the Hit Man collected twenty-five pennies and forked them over, Rinehart sat down on the sidelines to watch the game. He clapped. He whistled. He had this soft two-finger whistle he added to cheers: "Wheeeeo."

Zan listened to the whistle. She trapped the soccer ball with the inside of her foot and dribbled it. Rinehart whistled softer. Zan swooped down on the goal, aiming to score. She almost burst past the Hit Man. Ooooops, no! Down she went, hit by Randy. Oh, what good was Rinehart's wheeeeo, Zan wondered that day.

"Gotcha," said the Hit Man, stopping at Zan's fallen body. He took off his wool cap and wiggled it in her face.

"Randy got ya," said Fritz Slappy. He always sided with his teammate. He wouldn't know what else to say.

Eugene added, "I'd rot first before I'd lose a game to you." He stamped the ground near Zan's yellow hair. He had big feet, the biggest in his fifth-grade class.

Zan felt the earth shake. Getting up, she bumped into DumDum. "Aw," he said. "I dunno about you."

Randy and Fritz and Eugene and DumDum. They

called themselves the Mighty Four. They won games together. Autumn, winter, spring, summer—they cleaned up in every sport. Randy hit like a professional. Fritz hit like Randy. Eugene scared guys just by growling at them. He had a wicked temper. No telling what he would do if he got mad enough. And DumDum: he was taller than the other three put together, seemed like. Well—at least taller than any other player on the field.

The game began again. Randy scored again. Fritz flung his matching cap in the air. The Mighty Four surged toward the goal like one huge guy. Zan couldn't stop them. Her team couldn't. And she couldn't expect points from her own best friend. Rinehart sat watching from the sidelines calling "Waytogo, Zan!" and "Attaboy, DumDum!"

"Rinehart made a wrong mistake," DumDum shouted to Zan. "He cheered for me. I'm a enemy."

Eugene shook his fists in Rinehart's direction. "Butt out of our business or else."

"Wheeeeo," Rinehart answered.

Walking home from that soccer game, Zan felt grumpy. She hardly talked to Rinehart except to say, "Hurry."

Rinehart tried.

"Catch up, slouch."

Rinehart never caught up.

"Come on, Rinehart, do it."

In her mind Zan compared him to the Mighty Four. Rinehart couldn't walk as fast as Fritz could creep. Rinehart smiled instead of scowling like Eugene. Poor Rinehart couldn't scare a sparrow. He outsmarted DumDum in school, but he couldn't out-power him in sports. Rinehart the slouch, Randy the star. Never mind Rinehart's quiet whistles and soft hugs.

"Rinehart, I'm tired of being the only athlete in our friendship," Zan announced in front of his house. "I'm thinking of joining up with the Mighty Four."

"The Mighty Five," was all Rinehart said back.

Soon as Rinehart said "Five," Zan felt glum. Two is best, she thought. Me and Rinehart could be the Mighty Two if only he were mighty.

Zan looked at Rinehart standing there ready to say goodbye for the day. She already missed him, mighty or not. His glasses were steamed up from walking faster because she'd asked him to. The braces on his teeth made his smile shiny, she noticed for the first time. His best school pants had grubby grass stains where he had knelt down to cheer her from the sidelines. "Goodbye," Zan said sadly. "I'll miss your whistles like crazy."

"Goodbye," Rinehart agreed.

Zan took two slow steps away, then turned back to her pal. Rinehart hadn't moved. He seemed to be waiting for one last chance.

"I'll give you one last chance," Zan promised him and herself. She opened her sports notebook and showed Rinehart a list of all the sports he couldn't play. The list was long! Only one line was left blank on the whole page. "Rinehart, see this clean white spot?" Zan said. "I'm watching TV on Saturday afternoon. If I discover another sport you can't do, I'm writing it here. Then—then I'm switching my best friend to the Hit Man."

Rinehart studied Zan's list:

8

FOOTBALL
SOCCER
BASKETBALL
BASEBALL
SOFTBALL
VOLLEYBALL
BOWLING
PING-PONG
GOLF
WRESTLING
HIGH JUMPING
BIKE RACING
TENNIS

Rinehart nodded his head to agree that he couldn't play football . . . basketball . . . His head never stopped nodding. He ran his fingers down the page. "You're right. I can't play any of these."

He touched the empty last line.

"One last chance." Zan hurried away before Rinehart answered. She knew he'd say "Fine" or even "Lovely." He almost always agreed. That was one of the nicest things about Rinehart, that and his shiny smile.

She ran home fast to keep from thinking. Zan didn't like to think, except about sports, and she didn't want her brain to figure out any new sport on the Spectacular. Oh, anyway, maybe the TV would break. It's only Tuesday. Maybe a knob would fall off the TV by Saturday. If that happened, Zan couldn't change the channel from Saturday football. Football already led Rinehart's list. He couldn't tackle worth a darn. He could only be mauled.

Yes. Maybe a knob would fall off, Zan hoped a lot.

Arthur Rinehart   2

Arthur Rinehart was not Mr. Nobody. He knew that. He had the longest memory in his fifth-grade class.

He remembered his award for building the loveliest snowman in kindergarten. He remembered how he had helped his first-grade teacher tend their class greenhouse all year. He had learned to water plants faithfully and to keep them safe from cold corners. He got A in science. Also in behaving. He won the second-grade spelling bee. He remembered the dollar prize because he bought a plant of his own with it: his first fern. In third grade he bought other plants with money he won in the story-reading contest.

Rinehart's favorite memories were about Suzanne Hagen, his best friend he nicknamed "Zan."

She had transferred into his class last year. That same morning recess, Rinehart played his first soccer game. Zan had chosen him to make both teams have eleven players. When he said he'd never played before, she pressed her fingers to her mouth like a megaphone and promised loud to teach him. She also promised instant death if he didn't learn. Zan kicked hard and moved quick and never got winded. The Mighty Four decided not to like her then and there.

At noon she ate near Rinehart. She talked about nothing but sports. She seemed to understand a thousand different games. She knew about every superstar alive. She could even say what color hair and eyes her favorites had. After school she ran like them, scored like them, won like them. The Mighty Four changed their minds: they hated her.

Overnight Rinehart liked Zan best. He thought about why. He liked to think up reasons. He liked to think, period. Opposites attract is what he thought.

Zan scores; I don't.

I can spell; she can't, he thought.

She gulps; I eat slow.

I smile; Zan's serious.

She has blue eyes; my eyes are brown. Is blue the opposite of brown? Rinehart wondered about colors: about Zan's blue jeans and his brown pants; Zan's soccer shoes with white stripes and his plain brown school shoes.

Well, she's athletic and I'm not, Rinehart thought. By morning Rinehart believed that Zan could do anything he couldn't. Opposites attract, he was even more certain.

And vice versa. From then on, Rinehart helped Zan with her schoolwork so she could catch up to the class. He read to her at recess if she didn't finish morning lessons. He phoned her at night and read stories for hours. Each lunch they sat together. Zan ate with one hand and turned pages in her sports notebook. Rinehart loved looking at her star list.

BILLIE JEAN KING
MUHAMMAD ALI
PETE ROSE
LYNDA HUEY
O. J. SIMPSON
NADIA COMANECI
JULIE BROWN
JOE NAMATH
RANDY BOYLE

He memorized these names. That seemed fair to him.

"I wish your name was on this list," Zan always said during lunch. "I wish you could be an athlete." He wasn't learning a single soccer move in their games.

"I can make A's." Rinehart pointed out his opposite.

"Oh, please be athletic!" Zan's eyes were shining, so he knew she was serious.

Zan thought up a name to help Arthur Rinehart become a star. *Rinehart*, she named him. She knew tons of athletes on TV that announcers called by their last names. "*Rinehart*," she announced to their teacher. "*Rinehart*," she shouted on the field to the Mighty Four. She hoped they'd notice how sporty he became with his new name.

He remembered the name of every sports star Zan taught him. Words were easy. Playing ball was impossible. He couldn't figure out why Zan kept him for her best friend, unless opposites attracted her, too. As soon as she discovered he kicked like a slouch, well, why hadn't she dumped him? Instead, she tried to teach him another sport. And another. All during fourth grade. All during fifth grade, up to now, Rinehart remembered.

Having a good memory—being smart—made Arthur Rinehart Mr. Somebody in his classroom. Kids knew he wasn't a reading, history, geography, or science slouch. Far from it! He beat them on tests because he wrote answers fast. His pencil flew, even if Rinehart couldn't. He could multiply and divide in his head.

"You scored as many A's as I scored goals," Zan said about Rinehart's report card. She felt proud of him, sports slouch or not.

Best of all was when Rinehart read aloud in class. Zan forgot sports. It's true—she did. She loved Rinehart's voice gliding along sentences. She loved how he looked up at their class to laugh about the story. Oh, who cares if he can slug hits. The Mighty Four shut up for a change and listened. Rinehart never stumbled on words. He pronounced them right the first time, same as his teacher. He almost seemed to be telling the plot, not reading. He had this low, clear tone. He soothed kids. They listened forever. When the bell rang they almost didn't hear. Except the Hit Man heard. He said, "Come on, you all, ball-playing time."

Once on the field, Rinehart stopped being Mr. Somebody. But he always remembered he wasn't nobody. Hmmm. Perhaps Mr. Halfbody? And Zan the other half.

When Zan gave him his last chance that Tuesday, Rinehart felt gloomier than she did. Soon they wouldn't be best friends any more. Zan would see the Saturday Sports Spectacular. "Her list will fill up," said Rinehart to himself. "And I don't mean her star list." He slumped his shoulders and went into his house. He climbed slowly upstairs.

His room was crowded with plants. Every inch seemed green. And red, orange, blue, and yellow. Rinehart's plants had flowers on them, flowers in October. He could make them bloom even in autumn. He gave them plenty of air and sun from the windows. He watered them not too much, not too little. He cut off old brown leaves. And while he sprinkled plant food in the pots he talked softly. He said "Waytogrow," same as he called to kids playing soccer.

"Hang in there," he said today to a fern that had almost died once. He sponged its leaves with water. "Looking good," he said. He whistled at a droopy wild violet way over in the corner. He used his softest whistle.

Rinehart tended his plants every day after school. Sure, he was tired from falling down and walking home fast with Zan. But, exhausted or not, he cheered his plants so they'd grow flowers. He wanted every one to bloom at the exact same time. And he especially wanted ferns to bloom.

Rinehart smiled at them. "Ferns, you are beautiful. Please bloom."

They didn't. By reading books Rinehart learned that ferns weren't supposed to bloom. They were supposed to get taller and to spread out more. They would soon be wide, but they would never bloom, if Rinehart believed his books.

He didn't. He told his ferns, "Bloom, bloom," the way he told Zan, "Go, go," when she played ball. He made up this cheer for ferns:

Gimme a B. Gimme an L. Gimme a B-L-O— Gimme a B-L-O-O-M

At the end of his cheer Rinehart searched for tiny buds. Not yet, he noticed.

Rinehart sat down to watch his plants move. That sounds stupid. Most kids in Rinehart's school didn't know that plants can move by themselves. Rinehart found out by watching. He learned that plants move slowly. Plants turn slowly toward the sun to catch light. They grow leafier slowly. If Rinehart watched them an hour before dinner, he saw at least one leaf uncurl. Not quite like watching sports, but to him it was sort of like seeing his own slow self. His plants moved like him.

In the quiet of his room Rinehart thought about Zan. She'd phone him after the Sports Spectacular Saturday. She'd tell him her list had filled forever.

Then what?

Then Rinehart would need a new best friend.

But who? Kids in school didn't like him all that much, except when Rinehart read aloud or helped them on tests.

"Who?" Rinehart asked his ferns.

He already guessed who. He gazed around at flowers. Plants weren't swift like Zan. They weren't his opposites, except they were green and he wasn't. Zan would never write them on her star list. She didn't suspect he had all these pots full of friends. She didn't ask him what he played after soccer. Probably she thought Rinehart practiced falling down a lot.

"That's enough fresh air," he said to his future best friends.

He closed his windows. He moped about Zan's phone call Saturday. She would say "Skateboarding" for sure—her last line. Rinehart felt he would bust himself if he tried skateboarding. He knew he'd try, anyway. He'd borrow Eugene's skateboard.

Or Zan might say roller skating—skiing—Hmmm, he'd never learn to ski.

"Hmmm, maybe I won't answer the phone when she calls. Maybe the phone will break."

Rinehart sprayed a final drink on his ferns. He went downstairs to test the phone. He listened for a buzz. He dialed the operator. After Rinehart heard a voice he hung up in sorrow.

Hmmm. The phone has three full days to break. "Please B-R-E-A-K," Rinehart cheered.

Buster
Lifts

3

Zan liked the Saturday Sports Spectacular better than any other program. She always sat up close to the TV so she could see the stars' faces. She loved their crinkled eyes when they won. She knew just how they felt: happier than on their birthday. She loved when the winners told how they beat the losers. "We practiced harder," they said. Or, "I have a super coach who taught me how." One time a winner said, "This new racquet is my secret."

Sometimes Sports Spectacular showed team parties after the games. Players sang and squirted beers on each other. They wore towels around their necks. They wore their caps backward. Zan liked that part best.

Today Zan decided not to watch any part, not even the end to see winners. The living room stayed silent. Zan lay on the couch. She watched the clock instead of TV.

I've missed the music part, Zan thought.

A minute later she thought, I've missed the man who tells what sport it is today.

Zan rolled over to cover her head with a pillow. I don't care if I smother, she thought. The pillow smelled stale. The couch felt lumpy. Zan rolled off and crawled to the TV. Her hand shook turning knobs. Tears came to her eyes when she saw the bright picture.

"I'm doomed. It's the end of me and Rinehart." She wished she hadn't made her dumb threat about the empty line.

"And now, Buster will lift 500 pounds," announced a voice on TV.

Zan turned off the sound. She was afraid to hear a new sport. She lay face down on the floor. The rug got in her nose. She expected to choke to death any second, but choking seemed better than seeing Buster, whoever he could be. Buster Who? What sport could Buster play that was better than her pal? Rinehart reads faster and thinks faster and pats shoulders perfectly. What was Buster doing on TV instead of Rinehart? If only brains could be a sport!

Zan sat up to watch Buster, but he had disappeared. An advertisement showed men riding horses and smoking. Rinehart would fall off a horse, Zan knew. Also, he wouldn't be able to smoke a cigar. He'd cough and before that burn his fingers on the match.

"Lucky for me smoking isn't a sport," Zan hollered.

She turned up the TV sound. "Hurry up with the sports part."

Zan opened her notebook, ready to write whatever she saw. She licked her pencil point. She made an X on the last empty line. Right there it was curtains for her and Rinehart. Even though Zan wanted to stay friends forever with him, she would keep her promise—she always did. The announcer started to talk about Buster again—Buster this and Buster that. Buster could bend a steel bar with his bare hands. Buster could lift the biggest athlete in the world above his head. Once upon a time Buster had been a weakling with legs and arms thin as fishing poles. Just look at him now!

The TV glowed with Buster's strong body.

Zan looked closer at him. She groaned. "Rinehart can't swim," she blurted.

Buster wore a gold-looking swimsuit and nothing else, not even a backward cap.

"Rinehart can't dive, either," Zan said. She printed SWIMMING and DIVING on the last line. She rubbed her eyes on the pillow, thinking she might cry.

The announcer asked Buster, "How does it feel to be the world's strongest man?" Before he could answer, the announcer held up Buster's right arm so people could see how wide it was. Muscles rippled up and down that arm. Buster stepped away from the announcer. He went into a pose. He stood like a statue with his arms across his chest. His fists were big as cantaloupes. To Zan he looked more like a boxer than a swimmer.

Zan erased SWIMMING and DIVING and printed BOXING. Rinehart couldn't box anyone. He'd get punched in his smile. Anyway, Rinehart didn't own a swimsuit to wear fighting, or at least Zan had never seen him in one.

Wait a minute! Boxers don't wear swimsuits like Buster's. They wear baggy shorts like Muhammad Ali. This star Buster must be a wrestler. Zan suddenly got happy because WRESTLING was already on her list. She erased the last line, leaving only a gray smear.

"Rinehart's still my best friend forever until Buster plays his sport, whatever it is."

Zan said that while Buster posed. He turned from side to side. He held his hands on his hips and then moved his arms slowly up until he rested them on his head. He stooped down and whirled around at the same time. From the back you couldn't see past Buster. His shoulders stretched from one side of the screen to the other. His thick neck blocked out the announcer. Zan kept waiting for Buster to hop on a surfboard. But all he did was pose. Front, back, right side, left side. Stand tall, squat down. Pretty soon Zan had seen every muscle on his body.

POSING, Zan wrote on the gray spot. "What a strange sport. Even Rinehart can do that," said Zan. She erased POSING, leaving a hole on the list. Rinehart was safe until Buster got down to business and played his real sport. "After all, this isn't a Pose Spectacular," Zan told the announcer.

He announced: "Buster will today set an American record if he lifts 650 pounds."

Lifts? Zan didn't know that sport. Where is the playing field, she wondered. Where are the enemies— the other team? And why is Buster putting on his T-shirt? It says BUSTER across the front in gold letters. Whatever lifting is, Zan knew Rinehart couldn't do it. How could a sports bust be a Buster?

Lift? How could a kid with "hart" in his name do any sport?

Oh, if only being best friends were a sport by itself.

Buster bent over to lift an iron bar with round iron weights at each end. He lifted the bar up to his knees. He lifted it past his knees, past his stomach, all the way up to his chin. From his chin Buster pushed that iron bar over his head. He wasn't smiling any more. He squinted and grunted and said words like "Arg." His face turned pink on color TV. The pinker he turned, the more a voice announced, "Greatest LIFTER in America."

"*Aarrrgg,*" Buster said. He held the bar high over his head.

Right then Zan wrote BUSTER on her star list.

She began to catch on. Buster was playing weight-lifting. That must be a real sport, because Buster streamed sweat and tried with all his might to get better—to lift heavier weights. He set the new American record. Next he would set a world record. Athletes usually set records on Sports Spectacular, Zan knew. She paid attention to each move Buster made with the iron bar. She listened to the announcer tell how many pounds Buster lifted when he practiced every day.

Buster could crush the Hit Man, Zan thought. "Buster, you could slaughter the Mighty Four with one blow," she told her new star. Her notebook slipped to the floor. "Buster's really a lovely weight-lifter," Zan announced. She'd learned to say "lovely" from Rinehart.

21

"Buster is now Mr. Universe," added the official announcer. "Superstar of the weight-lifting world."

"Lifting," said Zan. She grabbed her notebook. On the last line she wrote:

LIFTING

She underlined this new sport twice.

Zan felt miserable drawing those two lines. Rinehart was such a nice guy. Where would she find a better friend to read stories to her? Rinehart could spell and—

He could lift! Rinehart! Lift! Any sports slouch could lift weights. Weights don't need to be thrown or caught or hit or bashed. All Rinehart had to do was bend over and pick weights up. Anyone with hands could lift. Plus Rinehart wouldn't stub his nose for a change.

Zan sprang to the phone. She dialed her favorite number. After around fifty rings a sad voice asked, "Skiing?"

"Rinehart, I've found your one last chance," Zan shouted. "I'm coming over to your house and teach you a sport I just now saw."

He didn't say anything. All the same Zan thought he sounded happy. She felt happy herself running to Rinehart's house on Glebe Road. He would still be her best friend. Also, he'd become her champion lifter. He'd get strong. He'd get to looking like Buster. Rinehart might even become Mr. Universe—Mr. Virginia—Mr. 1714 Glebe Road—okay, at least Mr. Somebody. One of these days Rinehart would outhit the Hit Man.

Lift Man

4

Rinehart lived at 1714 Glebe Road in Arlington, Virginia. Zan knew where because she walked him home every day after ball games. The house was a tall one with windows all around and a double garage, also with windows. Zan had been in the garage throwing balls to Rinehart on rainy days, but she'd never been inside Rinehart's house. He came over to hers to do her homework.

Zan rang his doorbell once.

And there stood Rinehart, smiling. "You ran here," he said to his pal. He looked to see what size ball she'd brought to throw at him. He held out his hands ready to catch.

Zan edged past Rinehart into the front hall. "I ran to teach you a sport that even *you* can play." Zan checked left and right for lifting space.

The living room seemed too crowded with couches for any sport except marbles. Where to lift? The dining-room chairs could be lifted into a corner. Start lifting, Zan thought. Then she noticed four corners full of other chairs. She followed the front hall to a kitchen. It's big enough, she thought. It's as wide here as Buster's iron bars. Could Rinehart lift in a room with pans hanging all over? Zan thought how cramped he might feel.

"Want a cupcake?" Rinehart opened the refrigerator. He passed Zan the cupcake with the most icing.

She said, "I don't eat before I play. Food makes me slow."

Oh oh, thought Rinehart. Zan plans to show me another ball I can't catch on the run. Must be in her pocket. Oh oh—the smaller the worse for me. I can't even catch a basketball.

Zan left the kitchen in a hurry. She opened doors along a hall. "A closet," she mumbled. "Another. You can't lift in a closet."

Lift? Lifting a ball sounded easier than catching one. Rinehart got cheerful again, until Zan started upstairs. "What's up there?" she asked, pointing.

"Oh oh," Rinehart said aloud. He couldn't help it. He meant that now Zan would see his plant collection. She'd learn about his ferns. She'd hate them for being slowpokes. She'd want to pinch them. She'd also hate Rinehart. She'd want to punch him. Opposites attract punches, he decided.

Zan took another step up.

24

She'll yell at my ferns.

Zan took two steps at a time.

Their leaves will wither, Rinehart just knew.

Zan bounded to the upstairs hall. She banged doors hunting for Rinehart's room. He sank down on the steps and held his ears. His ferns would never bloom if Zan hurt their feelings. They'd die instead. Rinehart laid his head against the wall. He thought and thought. He couldn't decide which was worse: losing his best friend or losing his next-to-best friends. Right then he couldn't decide why he even liked Zan in the first place. How could he put up with a fern killer? Opposites don't attract, after all.

Zan hollered down the steps, "Come up, Mighty Rinehart. I found us space for lifting together."

Oh oh. She's thrown my plants out the window, Rinehart convinced himself on the way to see.

Zan had changed Rinehart's room around. She'd moved his bed against a wall and his desk into a corner. She didn't say a word about his plants. She didn't seem to notice them until Rinehart whistled and said, "It looks huge as a golf course in here." He hoped Zan would like his "sports room."

"Golf course? I suppose you mean all these bushes," said Zan.

Rinehart knew she hadn't touched his plants. They were still alive, weren't they? He watched for Zan to pull a ball out of her pocket and whip a fast pass at his head. She liked to surprise him. He liked to be surprised by her strong throws, even if he always missed. Well, he wouldn't miss today, because a loose ball might conk a plant. He'd protect his friends.

He stretched his arms toward Zan. He spread his

fingers. "All the way," he said. "Throw." He tried to sound tough like the Hit Man, but Zan recognized Rinehart's usual voice. The soft sound drew her from her own secret thoughts. She'd been gazing at the plants and thinking, All these must clear out of here.

"Throw what?" Zan asked. She wanted to throw the plants—to make more lifting room. But she suddenly had another idea. "Lift this," she told Rinehart. She handed him a fern pot. Gently he took the pot from Zan's hands. He lifted it up near his face to smell leaves. That made him smile, made him hand that pot right back to Zan. She should smell green perfume herself.

"Take a sniff," Rinehart suggested.

Zan wouldn't. She was all business. She told Rinehart to lift the bush higher over his head. Lift it and then lower it. "That's right. Lift and lower. Lift higher."

Rinehart did as he was coached. When Zan handed him a bigger pot with a taller fern, he lifted that, too. Higher. Zan said, "Good lifting," and touched a bigger pot. Rinehart tugged it from the floor. He lifted it slowly. He said, "Arg."

His ferns seemed pleased with the slow ride Rinehart was giving them. They swayed toward him. He hadn't tended them this way before. Who knows, maybe if he played a sport with them they would bloom. Rinehart thought about blossoms at the same time he noticed how tired his arms felt. "May I rest now?" he asked Zan.

She answered, "Buster never rested on the Sports Spectacular."

"Buster? You mean you saw an athlete lifting

ferns? On television? Did he also water them? Did they bloom or anything?"

Zan didn't laugh at her pal. She always stayed serious about sports. For the next five minutes she explained weight-lifting to Rinehart. She made her voice sound important, like an announcer's.

"It's about bending over, grabbing the weight, and lifting it up—up—right over your head until your arms are straight. Bending. Grabbing. Lifting."

"What about catching?" Rinehart asked.

"No one throws anything."

"Hmmm." Rinehart's hum sounded happy. "What part does kicking play in this spectacular sport?"

"You don't kick weights. You'd kill your toes."

"Running? Jumping? Tackling?"

"No, none of those. Just bend, grab, lift," Zan promised.

"*Hmmmmmmmm.*" Rinehart's hum sounded like singing. Here was a sport he might do!

"The point is to lift more weight than other guys." Zan told what heavy weights Buster lifted and what Buster wore and how he screamed "Arg" like Rinehart just a few minutes ago. She ended up saying that Rinehart, star slouch, could lift if he tried.

Rinehart wasn't all that sure. For openers, he didn't own a swimsuit like Buster's or a shirt with his first name in gold letters: ARTHUR. He didn't own any lifting shoes with sticky rubber soles to keep him from slipping. Could he lift in his floppy galoshes? They were rubber. Could he wear his heavy jacket? That way, if he fell down, the pots wouldn't crush him.

"Wear anything you want, Rinehart. But you won't

be lifting your dumb bushes for long. We'll get real weights, the kind on TV. Monday we'll go buy them."

Rinehart listened to today's Spectacular over again. As Zan talked, he tended his plants. He lined them back up in rows near the windows. He knelt down to feel the dirt. The pots seemed damp enough. His room grew dark. Saturday afternoon turned into evening, Rinehart's loveliest time of day, because his plants smelled best then. Plants seemed to talk by putting out perfume, Rinehart noticed. "Smell this," he urged Zan.

She took a deep breath. She pinched the bushiest fern and smelled her fingers. "I don't smell a thing." Zan lifted and lowered that pot to Rinehart's rug. "One, two, three, four." She counted each lift.

"Five, six, seven, eight," Rinehart continued.

"Lift, Rinehart. Lift for me."

Two kids lifting ferns. Not exactly your Saturday Sports Spectacular! But Rinehart and Zan kept at it another half hour without complaining, either of them. Once in a while Rinehart said, "Smells lovely when this fern passes my nose." He inhaled and exhaled in a slow rhythm.

Zan didn't agree. But she didn't disagree. She wanted to know where the smells could be coming from, since Rinehart's ferns had no flowers. "Time out," she finally said. She switched on Rinehart's desk lamp. Under the light she examined her fern weight. "Where's the flower part?" she asked her pal.

"Ferns don't blossom."

Zan stared down at the plant on Rinehart's desk.

28

"Why not?" She lifted it once again. "Oh, anyway, so what? Who needs to lift flowers? Say, I wonder why plants just sit still."

"They may wonder why you rush around."

Zan almost smiled at Rinehart. Him and his jokes. Him and his flowers. "Those other ones have flowers." Zan waved at the wild violets, the begonias and at red, pink, and white impatiens—"I never saw so many kinds."

"I love them. They're my—" Rinehart wanted to say "Friends," but whispered "Teammates."

Zan said, "Some team." She started to say "Losers," but Rinehart sounded blue about his flowerless ferns. Zan watched him touch them with his slow-moving hands. His stubby fingers reached out to smooth leaves. Too bad those same fingers couldn't catch a ball.

Aha. They could lift. And Zan longed to teach them how.

"Time in," Zan said. She restarted them both, and while they lifted she asked Rinehart exactly why ferns wouldn't grow flowers. What the heck, other plants did.

She didn't believe Rinehart's answers. His book about plants was crazy. Zan promised that if Rinehart lifted every day with her and beat up the Hit Man and became a sports star—okay, check this out—she personally would make his dopey ferns bloom.

Rinehart seemed doubtful.

"I'll fix them up," Zan said to reassure him. "Your ferns will grow champion flowers OR ELSE."

Rinehart felt a pleasant chill under his collar and

29

his feet tingled in his galoshes. His smile came back once and for all today.

"Or else" was something Zan said if she really meant business. Rinehart loved nothing better than when she put on her stern voice for "or else." After that she would make it come true. She'd help him play ball, or else! She'd help him walk home faster, or else! And help she always did. Without Zan's teaching he would never even make it to the playing fields to watch her. Rinehart could go on and on with Zan's help.

Yes, sports were her joy—watching TV games, playing against the Mighty Four, teaching Rinehart—and here he stood, eager to please his best friend. In return she'd help his ferns bloom. She'd work her sports magic on them, he believed with his whole heart. In his same heart he held out hope he'd be good enough at this strange new game of lifting to feel the way Zan did about all her sports.

For now, Zan was leaving. Downstairs she reviewed their plans. They were buying weights Monday after school, then practicing every day until Rinehart could cream the Mighty Four.

"You'll get on my star list, ace," she promised. King, Ali, Rose, Huey, Simpson, Comaneci, Brown, Namath, Boyle; Rinehart and them.

Rinehart saw his name there already, along with Zan's own name. Together they'd be star bodies.

The Mighty Four and the Other Two

5

Monday afternoon on the soccer field: Rinehart and Zan were nowhere in sight.

The Mighty Four couldn't believe their eyes. They gazed in every direction. They blinked in the bright October sun. They scratched their heads right through their blue wool caps.

"Where are those two creeps?" asked Randy Boyle.

"Where?" echoed Fritz Slappy.

They looked down at their own feet and wondered. They were lined up on their same old playground, weren't they? This was their usual soccer time, wasn't it? So how come Zan wasn't here against them on the enemy team? And where could Rinehart be if

31

not on the sidelines fumbling his pennies and calling even DumDum "lovely"?

"The two of them musta died over the weekend," Randy decided at last.

"Croaked!" Fritz believed everything Randy did.

Eugene said, "They did us a favor. Our game will be better without both boobs."

DumDum wasn't so happy. "Nope, I never looked for this to happen," he told his teammates. "Rinehart wasn't all that bad. Dying's worse than losing, isn't it, Randy?"

"Not for me. Play ball." Randy began the soccer game with a powerful kick. He chased the ball hard. His henchmen tagged along to the net, passing to Randy when the ball came their way, helping Randy score Monday's first goal.

Randy and Fritz and Eugene and DumDum settled down to beat the stuffing out of a team that no longer had Zan as defender and Rinehart as hugger.

Meanwhile, Rinehart and Zan hung around the Arlington Sports Shop, asking questions about weights. Zan mostly wanted to find out prices. She could chip in her week's allowance for the next ten years, she told the salesman. She had no money with her at the moment. Rinehart carried his soccer penny donations in a flower pot. It was heavy as the weight of a fat black iron dumbbell.

The salesman told Rinehart, "Sir, to build your muscles you should buy a starter set of 100 pounds. Two dumbbells and one barbell, sir."

"How much will that cost?" Zan wanted to know.

Rinehart added the numbers in his head. He asked, "Do you deliver? I couldn't carry a hundred pounds to my house." Rinehart glanced at Zan with this promise: "I'll carry all these to China after a few months of practice." He smiled. He touched the weights gently. He ignored that they felt cold and hard, not a bit like his plants at home.

His penny collection paid for Rinehart's weights: $25.00 for 100 pounds. He and Zan rode in the delivery truck. They trailed upstairs behind a man who had piled the whole set of weights on one wide shoulder. He dumped two cardboard boxes on Rinehart's bed. He handed Rinehart a little book about putting weights together into a barbell and dumbbells. Rinehart had already read a chapter before the truck pulled out of his driveway.

While Rinehart read aloud from his book and Zan looked at the pictures, their enemies looked everywhere for them.

Randy and Fritz and Eugene and DumDum stomped along Arlington Boulevard. They searched different playgrounds. They noticed who rode in cars passing by. They went into Arlington County Library to ask if anyone had seen Turkey Rinehart or Meathead Zan. Eugene made up those mean names for his two enemies.

The Mighty Four had won their game all right, 6–0. But playing hadn't been any treat. They missed Rinehart's sad expression when Zan got pushed in a puddle. They missed Rinehart's calling "Please be careful" if they pushed even harder.

Randy was grouchy. What good was it being the Hit Man if he didn't have Zan to hit? "Where is she?" he asked his teammates.

"Where?" Fritz asked back. He flipped his penny, the one he would have given Rinehart to stay off field. "Nuts to him," Fritz insisted.

Eugene shouted that he had no one to shout at if Turkey and Meathead wouldn't play any more. "WHERE ARE THEY?"

DumDum barely kept up with the others. He was thinking, is why. He fooled along Military Road with his head slanted to one side. "Wait up, you guys," he said after a while. "In there's where Zan lives. I happen to know." DumDum nodded at a red brick house.

Randy made a fist and knocked at the front door. Fritz knocked again. Eugene pounded the door when no one answered and kicked a tree in the Hagens' back yard because he couldn't reach a window to peep in.

DumDum said, "I'm going home. I'll find them tomorrow in their desks."

"We'll find them now," Randy's voice snarled.

They all felt mean. They didn't know where to search next until Randy said, "Over to Rinehart's. Where does he live, DumDum?"

"I dunno." DumDum tipped his head.

"Fritz, where does Rinehart live?" Randy persisted.

Fritz seemed afraid to guess without a clue from Randy. Eugene was willing to follow Randy one more block and to punch telephone poles along the way. He punched a phone booth right before he had this idea: look up Rinehart's address in the phone book. He took charge. He paused. "What's Rinehart's last name?"

No one knew.

"I think it begins with some letter that comes near A in the alphabet," DumDum guessed.

Eugene said, "*Turkey* doesn't begin with A!"

34

No one laughed. The Mighties were too mad and hungry by now.

"At least I remember what Rinehart looks like in his dippy checkered jacket," Fritz offered with a hopeful nod at his captain. "I'll recognize him when we pass his house."

"Rinehart sure can read good," DumDum remembered. "And he taught me to subtract around three—no, two years ago." That memory made DumDum grin.

Eugene muttered, "All's I remember is when the turkey almost scored a goal for our team by accident."

"He walked the wrong way," Randy remembered.

But no one remembered Rinehart's last name.

"Mr. Rinehart," DumDum supposed.

Don't worry! They'd find Rinehart, name or not. They'd clobber him for skipping their game. Randy would see to that.

In the meantime, Arthur Rinehart and Zan Hagen had fit their weights together. On the bedroom floor lay two dumbbells. They each weighed 5 pounds. Next to them, stretching nearly across the room, lay the barbell with a 10-pound weight bolted to each end. The extra 70 pounds of weights were still in boxes, waiting for Rinehart to finish his beginning lifting program and begin the intermediate. Zan would add weights to the dumbbells and barbell as Rinehart grew stronger.

His room seemed more crowded than ever. Just since Saturday his ferns had put out new leaves, and with the boxes and dumbbells and impatiens around —whew. Zan shut her eyes and wished they had a bigger room.

She didn't wish long. She opened her eyes and saw out the window Rinehart's big garage with all its windows. They could carry the weights out there, and also maybe one or two ferns so Rinehart would feel cozy. There were shelves for his training galoshes and extra towels. They could drink from the hose. Yes, the garage seemed perfect. "How about it, sir?" Zan asked her pal.

Naturally Rinehart agreed to the garage, and not just because he was Mr. Nice Guy. He believed that his plants might stay healthier far away from his dumbbells. Warm leaves and cold iron don't mix, he told himself as he made the first trip downstairs. He lugged a dumbbell. Zan balanced the smallest fern on her head. She noticed how awkward Rinehart looked with the weight, not one bit like Buster.

Rinehart kept carrying the weights. He'd never make it to China, he thought. He huffed and puffed from his room to the garage with one weight each time. Much later he asked Zan to help him with the barbell.

"Aaarrrggg," they said together, tottering along the driveway.

So far, so good. Zan went back to Rinehart's room for other stuff and a flower. She set it next to the little fern on a workbench. Maybe the fern would learn how to bloom from the violet. That would keep her promise. Those plants seemed lonely away from the others. Zan opened a tall window to give them air and she turned on the light. No telling if plants saw the sun fading. Plants need light, she knew, from outdoors. Maybe they also needed a drink. Zan aimed the hose in their direction and let fly. "Bloom, guy," she told the fern.

At this very moment, the Mighty Four were prowling around Rinehart's back yard. They had found their two enemies by accident. From across Glebe Road they'd recognized Zan carrying Rinehart's jacket and something else, they couldn't see what. It might be a flower pot. Zan disappeared before they crossed Glebe.

When Zan turned on the light inside the garage, Randy crept to a window. Through it he saw Zan smelling plants. "Lookit, you guys," he whispered.

The Mighty Four peeked into the far window, and for the second time today they couldn't believe their eyes. In front of them stood Turkey Rinehart and Meathead Zan playing with flowers.

"I never took them for gardeners," DumDum murmured. "Can I go home now, Randy? I'm hungry."

On the other side of the window Zan touched a wild violet. She pointed to the other plant. She seemed to be asking questions, but the Hit Man couldn't hear what. He whispered, "I'd like to shove those pots down their throats."

"Ditto," whispered Fritz.

"Can you eat flowers?" DumDum asked so loud that the other guys ducked below the window.

They'd seen enough to make up their minds what was going on.

"Rinehart forced Zan to quit playing soccer and start up playing flowers so's I don't hit her anymore," whispered the Hit Man.

Fritz whispered, "You're right."

Eugene sneaked one more look in the window. "Zan's helping Rinehart buckle on his galoshes."

"There isn't any snow. They must be crazy," Randy snorted.

"Now Rinehart's lifting a long black thing and Zan's picking a leaf—"

"Nuts," Fritz muttered.

Hunkered below the window the Mighty Four listened to fast clapping coming from the garage. They heard Rinehart counting out loud. DumDum couldn't believe his ears. Could counting be a game? If so, he hoped he'd never have to play it.

All four boys were disgusted to death. Plus Dum-Dum was starving. He slipped away to his supper. Eugene growled, "I'll get even tomorrow," and followed. Randy decided he'd never miss a couple of gardeners in afternoon ball games. He'd hit other kids harder to make up. He'd pretty soon forget how often Zan scored against his team and how he liked to wreck her. He'd wreck something else. Ditto Fritz.

By tomorrow the memory of Rinehart's whistle would be fading from their field.

Rinehart and Zan Lift

6

Five . . . six . . . seven . . . eight," Rinehart gasped.

"Waytogo," Zan encouraged him.

"Ni-ne."

"Hang in there." She sat on the workbench and watched him closely.

"Arg. Ten."

"Attaboy, Rinehart."

Zan knew how to help keep him lifting. Every day in the garage she said exactly what Rinehart used to say to her on field. All those games he'd cheered— Zan'd memorized his words. She'd memorized his shoulder pats, too. When she saw Rinehart wanting to quit, wanting to drop the dumbbell and not to pick it up for a thousand years, Zan give him a fast pat.

"Five, six," he counted.

"Gimme an R-I-N-E—"

"Seven, arg, eight."

"H-A-R-T." Zan shouted her favorite part of her pal's name.

"Aarrgg—nine—"

"One more lift, Rinehart, just one more." Zan jumped to his side. She patted him on his jacket.

"Ten."

Rinehart put the dumbbell down on a shelf. He took off his glasses and wiped the fog with his sleeve. Zan gave him a towel to clean sweat off his fingers. She didn't want the weight to slip during his next set of lifts. Rinehart slumped against the garage wall. He didn't want to do his next set at all.

Zan knew how he felt. She'd often felt that way herself during an afternoon of soccer or basketball or baseball. Her arms had ached. Her legs had refused to take another step until Rinehart snuck to her side with a hug.

She hugged Rinehart now. She handed him the 5-pound dumbbell, saying, "Don't wilt yet. Only a few more exercises and we're finished."

Rinehart groaned but lifted again. "One, two, three, four."

He must count. He must keep track of how many times he did each exercise. Zan had written out a schedule in her sports notebook. Rinehart followed it daily with no skipping around in the order of lifts. No stopping at eight or nine, or nine and a half. Complete ten. Take some gulps of air, rest a minute, go on to the next exercise. No cheating. Just lift clean and think, Star list. Rinehart was serious about lifting his way up the list: "King, Ali, Rose, Huey, Simpson, Comaneci, Brown, Namath, Rinehart, Boyle," he chanted. Ten stars, ten lifts:

PRESS
MILITARY PRESS
ARM RAISES
SQUATS
DEAD LIFTS
BARBELL CURLS
WRIST CURLS
FLYS
SIT-UPS
LEG LIFTS

First came the press to strengthen his chest muscles. Then came the military press and arm raises to strengthen shoulders. Squats made Rinehart's legs strong; dead lifts worked on his back. Those were hard. They hurt like a fire spreading under his skin. Barbell curls weren't so bad until the ninth curl, tenth curl. Rinehart thought how strong his arms were getting, not about the pain.

And then wrist curls for wrists and forearms, flys for the chest, sit-ups and leg lifts for the stomach. And then? And then all over again next day after school: the presses, arm raises, squats, dead lifts; always in the same order, always ten of each. Days passed. The new routine became old and slightly more comfortable. Fun even. Rinehart moved himself up above Namath, without asking Zan.

". . . Brown, Rinehart, Namath, arg," he whispered to the barbell overhead in its military press.

Secretly Zan had already printed RINEHART above JULIE BROWN, her favorite runner on TV track meets.

Watching Rinehart work out, Zan noticed how his face glistened even brighter than Julie's racing face at the finish line. Also, he smiled lifting. Julie frowned worse than Eugene.

"Seeing you up close is better than those tiny guys on Sports Spectacular," Zan confessed one November day in the damp garage. "And every lift has an instant replay."

"Eight, nine, ten replays," Rinehart counted without a hitch.

Zan messed up his hair with a towel and told him how swell it was to have her own personal athlete to cheer from only a foot away. "Those Spectaculars don't listen to me," she griped. "I yell, 'Slam a homer,' and they bunt. I tell 'em, 'Serve your ace!' and they double-fault. You're smarter. You listen to what I coach."

Listen? Rinehart hung on Zan's instructions. That's how he had learned every lift so far. Today, in mid-November, his hands warmed with Zan's compliments. "You're taller than Ditto Fritz. I just now noticed," she said.

Then his hands warmed the iron barbells during his first set of lifts: ten presses. He lay on the garage floor face up. He held the barbell in both hands high over his chest. He lowered the barbell until it almost touched his chest. He pushed it up again. Lower and push. Count ten of these and go on to the military press. For this exercise stand up straight. Hold the barbell next to chest. Push it over head as far as possible. Lower the barbell and push it again. Count ten times. Drop the barbell, pick up a dumbbell for arm raises.

"Why ten of everything?" Rinehart asked on his

break. Zan was writing in her notebook and didn't answer.

Rinehart held the dumbbell in his left hand. Hold the left hand at side of body, he told himself. Slowly raise the dumbbell. Raise it higher than shoulders. Then lower it. Raise and lower ten times and change the dumbbell to right hand. Don't give up. Raise ten times.

"Why not five?" he almost pleaded.

He was in the middle of squats. "Five, six, seven, eight." He held the barbell on the back of his shoulders. From his standing position he lowered himself to a squat. "Ufff. Nine." He stood up again. He lowered himself to another squat. "Ten."

"Buster's book said ten," Zan finally answered him. "Buster says ten of each; you do ten."

Zan meant Buster's book named *Weight Training for Young Athletes*. Written by Buster. Pictures of Buster. Zan had taken it out of the library to show Rinehart how big his own arms would get someday, how wide his shoulders, how thick his neck with muscles.

"See Buster on page 20? He's how you'll look when you get old as him."

"Except for my face, of course." Rinehart laughed. "I'll still look like me. And the rest of Buster—all those muscles. I'll get that many only if I go on lifting for years."

Rinehart was almost finished with Buster's chapter called "Beginning Muscles." He had learned Buster's training tips for beginners: the best ways to warm up, the hand grips and foot positions, the proper ways to breathe.

"*Ten* dead lifts next," Zan said. Rinehart stood

tall, holding his barbell in both hands. He kept his legs stiff. He bent from the waist and touched his barbell to the floor. Stood up tall again, bent again, touching the floor with iron, again and again. "Ten," he said. "Anyone with hands can grip. A good gripper is a good lifter. So says Buster!" He mopped his forehead with a towel.

Zan poised her pencil to write "10" next to CURLS. She thought about Buster's first chapter, where he said anyone in the world could be a champion weightlifter.

Sure, anyone *could* lift. But not just anyone *would* lift day after day in a chilly garage without a team to lift alongside. And without enemies to egg a guy on.

Zan believed that the Hit Man would never train like Rinehart. Randy was playing basketball after school nowadays, him and his three henchmen. She saw them all in the gym on her way out of school. They hadn't asked Zan to play. They just yelled at her.

"Flowers," DumDum called across the gym.

She didn't know why.

Randy boasted, "I can sink a ball from anywhere." He grabbed the basketball and shot from the bleachers.

Swish. Fritz scored another.

"Your gardener can't shoot like that," Eugene yelled.

Zan already knew Rinehart couldn't even hit the backboard with a ball as big as China. But how— how did Eugene know about Rinehart's garden?

Oh, never mind how. Rinehart would scramble all

their brains with one punch each. Zan didn't miss her games against the Mighty Four. She liked coming home to their own secret gym. She liked coaching her flesh-and-blood Spectacular and announcing how Rinehart should lift, or else. She had tons of fun just erasing her star list to move Rinehart up. But, so far, the loveliest part of each lifting day was thinking how to get revenge on the Mighties. She told Rinehart, "They all must fall." Ali had said that one Saturday long ago.

The garage seemed colder than ever today in December. The hose dripped ice water. Windows were frosty. Would the two little plants on the workbench freeze to death before Rinehart became mighty? Zan circled their pots with her hands so the roots could warm up.

"Looking good," she said to Rinehart.

He continued his barbell curls. He held the barbell. He stood perfectly still except for his forearms. He moved the barbell up and down—from its first position across his legs to its highest position across his neck. Up, down. He counted, "Seven, eight."

"Looking lovely," Zan cheered to the fern, even though it didn't look so hot. Its leaves felt cold, she told Rinehart.

"Ten," he answered. "We need a heater near our plants."

Wrist curls came next on Rinehart's schedule. He did them with ease. Holding the barbell, he moved only his wrists. He curled them up, down. He counted and sweated. He grinned at Zan when she unbuttoned the top button on his jacket. She thought it might be strangling him. Breathing was hard enough for a lifter without such a tight collar.

Zan said, "If we had a heater, you could take off your jacket."

Rinehart counted his dumbbell flys. Flys were his favorites. He lay on his back. The damp garage floor dried up under him. He held his 5-pound dumbbells wide apart, at arm's length over his chest. Then he brought his hands together. The dumbbells clicked. He pushed his arms apart so the dumbbells returned to their first position. Then he brought his hands together again. "Two," he said, and, "Three, fourfive-six." His arms seemed to fly. He clicked the weights overhead like cymbals. He finished his set of ten flys with a bigger grin than ever. "Feels good," he exclaimed. "I'm catching on to why you love sports."

"Feels good? Only if you beat the other guys." Zan wished their enemies were here in the garage, lifting against Rinehart. She wished there was such a thing as a lifting contest. Rinehart would win.

Well, he might not. Zan remembered how it felt to be hit by Randy. She used to bounce a lot.

She remembered Fritz hit almost as hard.

Eugene has a strong mouth, she remembered. And DumDum. He can't keep score, but he's mighty and that counts. No, Rinehart was only a beginner. He wouldn't outlift those guys yet. They're all naturally strong. Rinehart better not deliver any Christmas punch.

Zan changed her wish. She wanted Rinehart's ferns to bloom. He'd kept his promise to her. He was lifting like a champion beginner. She'd have to keep her promise to him.

"Tomorrow I'll bring a heater from home," Zan

said in the middle of Rinehart's sit-ups. "I'll point it at this fern so it'll grow flowers." She blew her own warm breath on the little plant.

Rinehart was lying down, sitting up, lying down, sitting up. He pulled himself up with his stomach muscles. He held a 5-pound dumbbell behind his neck. It went up and down with him, ten times.

"You're almost finished your best workout ever," Zan encouraged. She ran her pencil along the list of Rinehart's lifts. She put "10" next to LEG LIFTS before Rinehart told her to. He lay on his back, moving his legs up and down. He was changing from a slouch into an athlete before Zan's very eyes.

"Ten," he said, not out of breath.

"Your lifts take up as many lines as my list of stars." Zan's hand shook with pleasure.

Ten exercises. Ten times each. $10 \times 10 = 100$. One hundred times today Rinehart had lifted his weights. And yesterday. And the day before that, way back to October. His muscles weren't sore. His joints weren't stiff. He didn't feel tired or hungry or bored.

He loved lifting, he confessed to Zan. "The minute my hands close over the barbell I feel like an athlete—how you must feel holding a ball. I love how weights sound clicking and thunking."

"I love how you balance them," Zan added. She rubbed his rosy cheeks with a towel. She helped him slough his galoshes off. She patted him here and there on his jacket. She couldn't feel a muscle under her patting hand. If Rinehart were growing some, they didn't stick up from beneath the wool.

Those two sat down on the workbench: Arthur Rinehart, captain and only player on their weight-lifting team. Zan Hagen, his spectator and fan. They moved closer to the plants. "Body heat will warm them up," Rinehart explained. Zan picked a violet and tied its long stem to the fern.

"There. I sort of kept my promise. It's a flower on a fern."

Rinehart said, "I sort of kept mine. I'm not Mr. Buster yet, but I've lifted all these chapters." He opened Buster's book. He found where he had to start lifting tomorrow.

Rinehart read softly: "Chapter 7. Intermediate Lifting."

"Sounds fun," Zan said.

"Intermediate lifters will lift 10-pound dumbbells instead of 5-pound dumbbells. They will lift 40-pound barbells instead of 20-pound barbells. All exercises will be done twenty times daily instead of ten."

Zan wrote "20" in her sports notebook. She erased SIMPSON and wrote O. J. RINEHART. Rinehart flipped through the pictures in Buster's book. Buster was doing his same beginning exercises and also new intermediate ones. Rinehart memorized the poses so he would know how to lift tomorrow. He read: "Intermediate lifters will follow this workout for two months."

Zan wrote that down. On her star page she drew a picture of Rinehart with muscles. She drew muscles on his jacket. His school pants had muscles where they stuck into the tops of his galoshes. Rinehart laughed at himself. "Are those muscles? Or flowers? Or what?"

"I can't draw," Zan admitted. "You can. Here."

Rinehart took the pencil. He drew a fern in his hands. He drew flowers on the fern. He said, "Anyway, lifting feels good."

The
Intermediate Man

7

But that was yesterday.

Today in the garage Rinehart groaned under his barbell. He struggled to press it off his chest and into the air. It felt so heavy with all those new pounds of iron attached. He felt so clumsy, like a slouch again after two months of being the Lift Man. He could scarcely press the barbell six times, seven times—

"What's the matter, Rinehart?"

"Nothing, Coach." He managed a weak sigh. He finished his ten presses and lay still. Then he remembered the ten more he must do for the first intermediate workout. He counted, "Eleven." He tried for twelve. Each inch his arms moved—up, up, up—hurt.

"Thirteen, fourteen." Zan took over counting. She watched her team struggle with the barbell. She almost leaned down to help Rinehart lift. That would be cheating, she knew, but at least Rinehart's eyes wouldn't say "Ouch." His face wouldn't be so purple. "Rinehart, let me help you off with your jacket. We have a heater. You'll be warm enough." Zan felt hot herself with the heater purring on her and the plants.

After his twenty presses, Rinehart lay still as a corpse. A beard of sweat clung to his chin. He had no energy to wipe it away or to stand up. Zan pulled him up. She hadn't done that since their old soccer days two months ago. She was worried. Her team seemed to be losing to the iron.

Rinehart could barely do his military presses. He wheezed. He got up to eight and slouched against the wall. He sat down after nine. It took him ten minutes to finish.

"Arm raises next." Zan handed Rinehart the dumbbell. She noticed how much heavier 10 pounds felt than his old 5-pound dumbbell. No wonder Rinehart raised his arm slowly . . . slowly . . . and practically dropped it to his side again. She counted to save him the trouble. On five he gave up.

Rinehart explained as soon as he caught his breath. He didn't want Zan to think he was sick. "Heavier weights and extra lifts are hard on the muscles," he said.

Hard? Make that vicious, Zan thought.

He pulled back his jacket sleeve so Zan could see his wrist. He clenched his fist. His wrist muscle poked up. "This muscle—all my muscles—will grow only if I lift heavier and heavier weights. Lift them more and more times. Otherwise I'll just stay the same."

Zan wanted to see what Rinehart meant by "the same." What did the rest of Rinehart look like? He always wore his goofy jacket and long pants. His braces covered his teeth. His glasses covered his eyes. Zan decided to check out his hair. It's brown. She'd remember that for her star list, like Pete Rose's hair. "Help me get this straight, Rinehart. Hair doesn't have muscles. Or does it?"

"Not according to Buster's book." Rinehart placed the barbell behind his neck so it sat firmly on his shoulders. He held it there for three squats, four squats. Even though he'd rested, squatting felt terrible. Pain shot through his legs. Each squat cost him a moan.

Zan felt sorrier and sorrier for her pal. During his dead lifts she couldn't watch. She looked at the fern instead. She listened to Rinehart complain every dead lift.

"There's too much heat. I'm on fire," he murmured. "Too much heater."

"There's a draft coming under the garage door. I'm numb." His soft voice faded.

"My jacket itches."

"But I need padding if I fall under the barbell." His voice trailed off into a whimper.

Zan had never heard Rinehart complain. He must be hurting something fierce. She couldn't decide how to help him. He must lift his own weights to grow muscles. His coach couldn't lift for him. All Zan could do was cheer and hug and whistle, erase and announce. How else could she make him comfortable as he lifted the vicious weights two hundred times today?

Rinehart whispered, "I can't do one more curl," after his first one. He sat stiller than his plants. In the long time he rested Zan watched their two plants bend toward the heater.

Ferns, Zan thought. All his ferns and other plants. His teammates! Rinehart needs all his teammates for company. He needs a rug under his back during presses and flys. He could use cupcakes for energy. And enemies—they would force Rinehart to try even harder. He needs the Mighty Four to lift against.

Rinehart was only thinking, I need to rest forever.

Next morning Zan raced over to Rinehart's house instead of to school. Lucky—no one was home. Rinehart's mom drove his father to work at the same time each day: 8:00 a.m. Zan found the extra key under a doormat and let herself in. She found cupcakes in the kitchen and a rug in a bathroom. She carried her loot outside, opened the garage door, and went in to arrange Rinehart's gym.

Upstairs in his room again Zan found his teammates. How they'd grown in the two months Zan hadn't seen them! She staggered under the weight of their million leaves and spreading flowers. Each trip downstairs she decided would be her last, but of course Zan didn't quit until the entire team sat in the gym in their pots.

There now. Everything to make Rinehart comfy, everything except enemies.

Rinehart needs someone to lift against, Zan

thought. It's so much fun to beat other guys. Zan remembered her own soccer goals, how swell her foot felt blasting past Randy, past Fritz. "I'd feel even sweller if Rinehart could lift more pounds than those meanies." Zan said that to a fern. She held a pot tight and jigged here and there.

One by one Zan danced the ferns into a circle. With each step she planned how to make the Mighty Four come on over for a lifting spectacular.

She'd phone them. No, Eugene would break her eardrum with a growl.

She'd write notes. She'd leave them on their desks. Sure, if only DumDum could read.

Suppose today at recess she zipped right up to the whole Mighty Four and explained lifting. Randy would say—

No good.

Randy wouldn't say. He hadn't spoken to Zan since their last soccer game months ago. He'd forgotten she was in school. Fritz dittoed the silence, and the other two guys yelled "Flowers, hahaha" when the lifter or his coach sat near them at lunch.

"Flowers, pass the catsup," demanded Eugene.

"Can you eat catsup on flowers?" DumDum mumbled.

Then Eugene yelled "Flowers don't count," yelled "Flowers can't score," yelled "Flowers just croak." Flowers from the meanies and nothing more!

There now. Zan had finished arranging the ferns in a huddle around Rinehart's garage rug. He'd lie on it this afternoon. He'll love the soft floor. He'll do his twenty presses. In two more months he'll finish his Intermediate Program. He'll be stronger than

Randy. Ha ha. The Hit Team will wither alongside Mighty Rinehart!

How to lure the Feeble Four inside the garage so they'll start fading?

Not to worry. Zan would think of a way. Just as she thought up how to make Rinehart's ferns bloom. Just like this—zingo.

She pulled a small package from her back pocket. Here's the best part of making this garage snug, she decided. She'd spent hours last night cutting note-book paper into flowers. These blue-and-white-striped blooms would make Rinehart smile instead of complain. Zan glued them on the ferns with Elmer's glue from a garage shelf.

"Surprise!" she said, and ran off to school.

"Let's go straight to our garage," Zan mentioned after school that same day.

Rinehart dragged his feet along Glebe Road. Honest, he had no strength for lifting. His poor sore body told him to give up on weights, to find another sport that wouldn't hurt so much. He tried to lift his empty lunchbox overhead. *"Aarrgg"* was his only comment.

"You'll feel better after a few warm-up exercises," Zan reminded him.

All the way home Rinehart complained: "It's cold. It's windy. It's going to snow."

"It's December," Zan said matter-of-factly.

He complained a lot more, but once he saw the garage greenhouse Zan had fixed up, he went to work lifting. He owed his coach the effort. He loved the ferns blooming with paper flowers. Zan had kept her promise. Now he kept his by unbuttoning his jacket and following his schedule. He couldn't lift as smoothly as before, he couldn't lift as fast. He paused and licked the frozen hose and nibbled a snack.

Zan peeled the paper off his cupcakes. She tended the plants. At the slow rate Rinehart was lifting, he'd have no time to cheer his ferns before dinner.

His arms throbbed. He got an awful stitch in his side. His eyes filled with tears at eighteen, nineteen, twenty curls.

Yet Rinehart found a way to keep on lifting. As he moved the weights he concentrated on his goal: to become a stellar athlete so he could understand his best friend inside out. Rinehart concentrated on strength. In his mind he saw his own muscles. Oh oh, they hurt. That meant they were working hard. Working meant they were growing bigger. Rinehart thought about the pictures of Buster's muscles. He thought how his own muscles were in the same places as Buster's, only not as big.

"I'll have to grow mine more. I'll lift and lift and lift. King. Ali. Rose. Rinehart." He muttered the star list lifting.

When Zan spoke to him, he wouldn't answer, not even during his rest breaks. He was concentrating with all his might. She gave up and talked approvingly to their plants. She told every fern they reminded her of Rinehart, so quiet and all. No wonder she liked them. Why wasn't Rinehart green, too? Maybe his eyes were. Zan checked through his steamy glasses. She saw brown to match his brown hair.

It was dark outside, time for the plants to put out

perfume. Zan drew in her breath. She smelled only notebook-paper flowers. Rinehart couldn't notice smells. He had all he could do with flys. The dumbbells looked more like they were trudging through air, not flying. Zan saw Rinehart's neck muscles straining as he brought the dumbbells together with a clank.

"*Help*," he admitted.

Zan helped with a "Lovely, Rinehart."

His neck and wrists were all Zan could see of Rinehart's new strong body. But she believed with all her mind that down under his jacket, his shirt, his pants, and his galoshes Rinehart was growing intermediate muscles. She'd brag about them to Randy—how rock hard, how tough Rinehart was getting. Randy'd be furious. Aha, wait'll his Hit Team tries to hit us.

The
Hit Team Hits

8

In January, when Rinehart had half finished his
Intermediate Program, Zan went hunting for the
Hit Man. She found him shooting baskets in the
school gym. He seemed bigger than he used to be
playing soccer. He wore shorts and a tank top that
showed him off. Zan was impressed. His name,
RANDY, covered his chest in blue letters.

He reminds me of Buster, Zan thought.

No, Rinehart is Buster, and he will beat this guy
up. Zan kept thinking as she walked up to Randy.
He didn't stop shooting. Balls plopped through the
rim. Fritz caught and threw them back to his captain.
Eugene practiced scowling from basket to basket,

looking meaner than ever. DumDum looked taller than before as he counted Randy's baskets.

"One, one, one." DumDum seemed sure of that.

Zan acted as if she wasn't afraid of them. She said, "You guys—"

"No way you can play on our team," Randy answered for them.

"Randy, listen up," Zan insisted.

"Can't play against us. And wherever that *turkey* is, he can't hang around our gym earning money."

Fritz nodded his ditto.

Zan said, "Randy, you come over to our gym. Try to play our new sport. Over in Rinehart's garage on Glebe Road."

"What sport?" Randy never took his eyes off his swishers. "Hide-and-seek?"

"Ha ha ha." Three laughed. One stayed busy counting up to one.

Zan answered over their rowdy backslapping: "Rinehart is lifting. It's a sport I saw on TV."

"Never heard of lifting. You must get freaky channels."

"Channel W-E-I-R-D-O," Eugene announced.

Zan wouldn't give up. She leaped to catch a rebound. Holding the basketball in both hands, she said, "Lift—like this." She managed to push the ball overhead before Fritz grabbed it.

"One," DumDum counted. "One lift."

Fritz passed to Randy, Randy to Eugene, Eugene to DumDum, DumDum to Fritz. No one shot a basket. They giggled and lifted. "Like this?" Fritz asked, lifting the ball with one hand. "Like this?" Randy balanced the ball on one finger. Eugene lifted the basketball with one toe and aimed his kick at Zan. She caught it on an ear.

"Beware. Rinehart is the Mighty One," Zan called, backing away from the bullies. She fled the laughter-filled gym.

In February Zan tried again.

Rinehart was beginning his Advanced Program. A lifting contest today would be fun for him to win, Zan figured out on her way to the cafeteria for lunch.

The Hit Team laughed longer this time. "Lifting? Like this?" Randy took a Twinkie in each hand and lifted them as far as his teeth. Fritz wasn't so strong: he lifted a pea until it spilled from his spoon. Good-bye lunch.

Zan tried all afternoon. She passed Eugene a note saying, "You can *beat Randy* at lifting!!!" He sent it back as a spitball. The note for DumDum said, "Be the #1 lifter on your team." Zan read it to him at recess.

"Aw, I couldn't lift Randy and Fritz and Eugene—those two guys," he whispered.

After school the Hit Team took over the gym. Zan shouted cross-court, but they couldn't hear her sentences, only the words "sport . . . lift . . . contest . . . garage . . . Rinehart . . . win." They saw Zan lifting her books, her coat, one end of a bench. She pretended to lift the bleachers. The boys began to wonder what else.

Zan thought she heard their footsteps behind her on the way over to Rinehart's.

But Randy and Fritz and Eugene and DumDum didn't budge from their court. They played their usual winning game together. Afterward they fooled around trying to outscore each other in a pick-up game from the foul line. Randy won it. He always won. Fritz came in second. There was no third place because DumDum lost track of his shots and Eugene quit in a funk and let the air out of every basketball. He hated to lose, even to his captain. His mood changed from worse to dreadful.

All this time they wondered about Turkey's new sport. What could it be?

"Lifting what?" Fritz asked.

"Some kind of a ball," Randy predicted. He'd never played a sport without a ball.

In the locker room the Four Mighties changed their clothes wondering. "How many Ping-Pong balls can you lift?" DumDum asked Randy.

"Nine million easy," Randy shouted.

Nine million sounded like a lot, maybe more than tons. DumDum was impressed. "Let's all go over there to Rinehart's and lift nine million."

Eugene left the gym grumping about how he'd like to wring a turkey's neck. No way Rinehart could beat him at anything except reading and arithmetic and—

"Those don't count," DumDum said.

"Rinehart's a goner," Randy boasted. He flexed his forearm. Muscles showed when he pushed his sleeve back.

Ditto Fritz's.

Eugene cracked his knuckles. He said, "I'm going over and total that garden right now." DumDum concluded, "It's us against them. I dunno—three against zero."

The Mighty Four headed toward Rinehart's garage.

They couldn't care less how cold and late it was already. Let supper wait. So what if the February wind blasted their ears? They pulled down their matching caps. They looked like a bunch of punks crossing Arlington Boulevard.

Running along Glebe Road, they bragged about what meanies they were. "I got back at my brother for messing up my clothes. I messed him up," Randy led off.

Fritz couldn't say ditto. He didn't have a little brother. He had to brag, "I pushed my sister over."

"In fourth grade I stiffed the whole class for calling me 'Genie.'" Eugene hated his nickname. DumDum didn't like his nickname, either. But heck, he couldn't stiff the first grade, second grade—he couldn't count up to the other grades. He muttered his real name, Walter. He wished he had a nifty shirt like Randy's: WALTER it would say in tall letters.

Rinehart's garage was dark when the Hit Team arrived. No wonder, at 7:00 p.m.! Rinehart was in his house eating. He felt exhausted after his first advanced workout. He'd lifted 20-pound dumbbells thirty times each exercise. His barbell now weighed 50 pounds.

And Zan had gone home to supper after Rinehart quit. She couldn't wait all night for the Hit Man. She hadn't told Rinehart about her challenge because she wanted to surprise him. Rinehart loved surprises.

Okay, get ready for one!

Randy tried the garage window. "I can't see a thing," he whispered. He wanted to break the glass. Eugene came up with a better idea—bash down the door. He whispered, "All together. One, two, three—"

The door opened easily. Fritz tripped and took a

header. He landed on the floor but not on the bathmat. He skinned his knees. So did Randy from bumping the wall. Eugene fell against the workbench, causing flower pots to rumble. DumDum tiptoed into the garage. He'd missed the number to bash.

All four Mighties rambled around in the darkness. They touched everything to make sure their enemies weren't hiding. They found plants but no people. They didn't touch surfboards or hockey sticks or bikes. No new creepy sports, like Zan said.

"Unless this garden is a sport." Randy pretended to be throwing a ball. He aimed a pot at Fritz's shadow—and boom.

That pot broke. The plant lay buried in its dirt. Randy broke another pot by dropping it on the cement floor. He slam-dunked a pot into a trash can. POW. He discovered big pots in a circle around something soft on the floor. He tipped these over with a flick of his foot. "Come on, you guys, join my new sport." He touched pots on the workbench. He spiked one of them like a football in the end zone. He strutted.

Pots were bombs to Randy. Leaves were there to be picked and scattered on Rinehart's weights. No one saw those weights. The dumbbells sat on pitch-black shelves. The barbell was only something cold and unmovable on the floor. Eugene stubbed his toe against it. He hopped around cussing Randy. Randy stunk for dragging him into this hot old garage. Randy this and Randy that. Eugene sat down to nurse his toe.

"I'll rot first before I'll play garden."

"Then rot," Randy snapped.

Eugene sulked. DumDum kept on holding the huge

plant he meant to toss down. It smelled so good. A flower lay against his nose. Leaves pushed their way up his cheeks. "Aw," DumDum said, "this tickles."

"Throw it," Randy commanded.

DumDum couldn't bear to let go of his treasure. It seemed to be hugging him back, just as Rinehart used to hug him at games. DumDum buried his face in his plant and cruised around the garage. His foot nudged the barbell. He stepped over it lightly. He hummed in time to his dance. When his arms soon got tired, he set his plant down near the heater, where he'd found it. He knelt to bite a few leaves. They tasted as good as they smelled. DumDum was hungry.

You would think that Ditto Fritz was there smashing pots alongside Randy.

Nuts to that. Fritz pulled plants up by their roots. That was easier than throwing them anywhere. The heavy pots took too much lifting energy for a guy who was tired from basketball. Fritz twisted flowers off their stalks. After many handfuls of soft blooms he touched flowers he could tear exactly in half— tear into pieces, like paper.

"Lookit, Randy. These real big ones grew paper flowers. There's something magic going on in here."

"I can't see. Find the lights." Randy had run out of pots to throw. He began kicking pieces against the walls.

Searching for lights, Fritz bumped into Eugene's stubbed toe. That started a fight. The teammates rolled back and forth in paper petals. Their caps came loose and were lost in cobwebby corners. Now they snatched each other's hair.

DumDum liked the dark. He roamed the shambles,

taking bites of different leaves. He touched along the shelves for something to drink. He never found the hose. He stuffed ferns in his pockets to show his mom. Yep, she might want some for her salad. He groped his way out of the garage and hurried home.

So did the others.

No one on the Hit Team turned on the lights in Rinehart's garage that evening. They missed enjoying their own wreck. They missed finding the sport Zan had invited them to play against Rinehart. They missed seeing their mean, dirt-smeared selves in the full-length mirror that hung near the door. Zan had brought it over from her house because Rinehart had asked for a mirror. He was getting very fussy. He wanted to watch his hand positions on the weights. He planned to watch each new lift in the Advanced Program.

Rinehart would compare himself to pictures of Buster. He'd look in Zan's mirror and see his body for a change, instead of seeing his clothes. He'd see ARTHUR.

Arthur

9

"**A**t least our mirror is still in one piece."

Rinehart's soft voice comforted Zan. She had been crying ever since they found their ruined gym.

"And the heater didn't get unplugged," she blubbered. "But our plants—Wreck City." She blew her nose on a dead paper flower.

Rinehart hadn't even sniffled. That's because of the shock when he'd opened their garage door. His face went white, not crimson like Zan's. His eyes went empty, not full of tears. His feet froze to the floor, even with the heater on.

Down under Rinehart's checkered jacket and school shirt and undershirt and skin and flesh, his heart nearly broke in two.

"Please don't break," Rinehart cheered it.

It broke anyway.

But then he remembered that a heart's a muscle—one of his body's six hundred muscles. His heart was as strong as his fist from all his lifting. Hearts and fists are the exact same size, Rinehart knew from the pictures in Buster's book. And his fist simply didn't break.

Yes, but Rinehart's heart broke.

He opened the book and turned pages to the Advanced Program. "Heart, don't break any more, don't." He groaned a cheer, "Gimme an H."

Besides cry a lot, what could Zan do about this wreck?

Fix it up, is what. Not with Rinehart's help, either. He must go on lifting today—they both agreed after Zan begged him to. He must not diddle his time away. Zan would clean up, she promised. She would start by finding Rinehart's barbell where he had left it the afternoon before.

With a towel she wiped dirt off the barbell. She tried to pick it up, but the 50-pound barbell wasn't about to lift for her. Rinehart had to rescue it from heaps of broken pots. He snatched it from the floor to the position of his first exercise. He counted the times he snatched the barbell off the floor, lifted it, and set it down. "Snatching" was the name of his first advanced lift.

"Arg. Arg. Arg." That's how Rinehart counted today while Zan swept. Her broom moved slowly because her hands slipped on tears. She worked carefully around Rinehart's galoshes. Not to disturb him! He must keep lifting so he'd be strong enough to beat up whoever made this mess.

In one quick move—"Arg"—Rinehart snatched his barbell from the floor and lifted it over his head. He watched himself in the mirror. He'd taken off his glasses to wipe tears away. So far he looked funny to himself.

Zan shook the mat. She laid it back down on a clean patch of cement. She turned the ferns right side up that Randy had tipped over last night. They were still planted in their pots and looking fine, except that all their paper flowers had been torn off, plus some leaves. But the other plants! Dead, looked like. Zan started to sob. Oh, who could have killed her real, live flowers? She glanced at Rinehart in the mirror for an answer.

He was absorbed in his moves, or at least he pretended to be. He watched his neck redden above his jacket collar. His face muscles tightened as he held the barbell overhead. On his tenth snatch Rinehart gritted his teeth. His braces glinted in the mirror. He blinked at her.

"Hmmm," he said. He counted snatches. "Hmmm. Hmmm."

Zan finished sweeping the center of their gym. "Now for the rest of this mess," she said. Someone had to talk in Wreck City. Her broom jabbed two dirty caps. "Whose?" She never wore a cap, and Rinehart wore earmuffs.

He sat on the floor resting. He had his earmuffs off now for a change. Also his jacket. He touched his forearms through his shirt. He asked Zan, "Do you remember those matching caps Randy and Fritz and Genie and Walter wear to play soccer?"

"Those murderers!" Zan wanted to run back to school and catch all four in their basketball game.

She'd fix them up. She'd go there as soon as she gathered her dead plants. First she'd hold a funeral for them. She'd bury the begonias, impatiens, and oh these poor tamed violets—she'd—

She'd fix *them* up.

Zan turned to Rinehart to ask how to save their plants. He stood thumping his heart through his shirt, as if to make sure it wasn't broken.

"Rinehart, their roots aren't frozen so I'll plant them again."

"Lovely," he said, and started lifting. He watched his bare forearms in the mirror. He had rolled back his sleeves. Same here, Zan thought. She rolled hers up. She'd think of where to plant the half-dead flowers. She was getting used to thinking. She was growing used to moving around the greenhouse slowly, gathering uprooted violets, thinking aloud.

"Gently smooth the leaves."

"Dampen them."

"Easy."

"Attagirl."

"Dig holes for them in these big fern pots in a huddle. There's room for small plants under the tall ferns. They can grow together." Zan smiled, replanting the half-alive flowers. She waved her dirt-brown hands at Rinehart. Someone had to be cheerful around here.

Zan dragged her huge fern pots to the empty workbench. She put every pot up there so the heater could blow a hot breeze across that line of green. Afternoon sunlight came through the tall windows, making her repotted plants look alive. The ferns seemed healthy as ever.

"Too bad these ferns didn't have thorns yesterday. Thorns would've stuck the murderers."

Thorns are lovelier than flowers, Zan thought when Rinehart didn't answer with some revenge scheme of his own. She caught his eye in the mirror. "I promise to make our ferns grow thorns if you promise to take care of the Hit Man and them."

Rinehart was so busy keeping his original promise to Zan he couldn't make another right that minute. In two more months he'd finish Buster's Advanced Program. Each day of training between now and April was important. Rinehart hoped to turn the last page of Buster's book and be a real weight-lifter. Not as big as Buster, not as strong, not as old. But he'd be the athlete he'd tried for six months in a row to be.

In front of the mirror Rinehart lifted his last barbell today. He set it down with a "Hmmm." He socked his heart one last time. He took off his school shirt. He stretched his arms toward the mirror. His strong fists touched glass. No doubt about it—his forearms were wider than last October, when he had started lifting. He took off his undershirt. He posed a Buster pose. His chest and shoulders gleamed with sweat. Under the beads of water Rinehart saw his broader, fuller chest; his wider, muscular shoulders. "Lifting works," he exclaimed.

Surprise City.

And Rinehart loved surprises. In the mirror he compared himself to Buster. He turned around to see his back with muscles popping up as he raised his arms. He turned sideways. He slapped his stomach: hard as the cement floor.

"Slap Randy like that!" Zan had heard Rinehart's

slap. She wasn't watching him. She still tended their plants. She stopped tending at the same time Rinehart kicked off his galoshes. He hiked up his school pants above the knees. Zan came over to the mirror and announced: "Buster."

Rinehart was naked—well, almost naked. Except for his rolled-up pants and his teeth braces, he stood there uncovered. And he was no slouch.

Believe it!

Four months of lifting had built muscles everywhere Zan checked him. He flexed his legs: muscles rippled in ridges. When he bent an arm at the elbow, muscles jumped right up. When he turned his head, muscles stood out from his neck.

"Arthur," Zan hollered.

She found a towel. She shook dirt from it and draped it around his neck. "You're the star of Sports Spectacular," she sang out. She slung his checkered jacket around his shoulders and tied the woolly sleeves in a knot around his crimson neck. "Your dopey warm-up jacket." She laughed and gave him a hug. "Billie Jean King, Muhammad Ali, Arthur Rinehart. You'll get our revenge. You'll destroy our enemies."

Rinehart didn't agree. He never did with her revenge plans. He only said, "I must finish Buster's book. I'll do every lift he describes. If I stop lifting—now or ever—I'll shrink right back down to my same old self. Muscles fade if you don't keep working them. So says Buster."

He knew the Advanced Program would wear him out again tomorrow. But he also knew that in time his body would be powerful. He would catch up to the heavier weights. They'd feel lighter every coming day.

"In two months I'll—hmmm—maybe I will beat them," Rinehart said in his usual soft voice. A threat sounded strange coming from him. He posed again with his legs wide apart and his arms crossed against his chest. He didn't look strange. He looked strong.

"Beat them *up*," Zan agreed.

"Beat them *out*. At weight-lifting." Rinehart explained his scheme. "In a contest. Me against them, one at a time." He tensed his arms as if he were lifting.

Zan said, "There's no such thing as a lifting contest in Arlington."

"We could have one."

"How?"

"Invite them over here." Rinehart patted his barbell.

"I already invited them yesterday," Zan admitted. "See what happened?" Still more tears came into her eyes.

Rinehart didn't crash about his wrecked gym. He looked in the mirror. Behind his firm, broad shoulders the garage came into focus. He saw how neatly Zan had fixed it while he had been working out. He recognized their ferns alive on the workbench. He put on his glasses and noticed the little plants that used to blossom. They were planted in the same pots with ferns, under the big arching fern leaves. They didn't have any buds or blooms now, but Zan was trying to save them, anyway.

And she came into focus in his mirror. She stood behind him, brown with dirt, covered with live green leaves. Her yellow hair stood in tufts. Her blue eyes crinkled as Rinehart explained about their lifting contest. She nodded fast, agreeing with his plans. She bent toward the mirror, silently listening. Zan looked like a flower to Rinehart in his greenhouse. Then and there he put her on his star list:

ZAN HAGEN
ARTHUR RINEHART

"Zan, I'll bring chairs out here from the house. We'll build a stage. Eugene will be our welcoming committee. You'll be the announcer and read from your sports notebook."

Zan joined the planning. "You can wear your earmuffs backward when you win."

"Walter will add up the scores of each lifter."

"You'll squirt us with the hose when you win." Zan knew a hose could squirt harder than bottles of beer.

"Fritz will— Who knows what Fritz will do at our contest?"

"When?" Zan asked. "When will our Lifting Spectacular be?"

"In April, after I come to the last page of Buster's book." Rinehart ended with a "Wheeeeo."

Zan told him, "Arthur, lifting hasn't made your whistle any stronger."

Mr. Arlington **10**

Arlington County lay sound asleep when Dum-Dum jumped up that Saturday morning in April. He couldn't mess around in bed. He had important things to do. DumDum was getting ready to be Mr. Arlington.

He wanted badly to win. Mr. Arlington would get a shirt with his name on it in gold letters, Zan had told DumDum in school. He usually didn't go around listening to Zan, but she had a good idea there. His winning shirt would say WALTER.

"Yep," he yawned, lifting his feather pillow. He wandered across his bedroom lifting all his junk: two tennis balls, an empty goldfish bowl, his blown-up balloon collection, his snack bag full of marshmallows. Zan had urged him to practice lifting weights because Mr. Arlington would be the best lifter in Rinehart's garage today. Mr. Arlington would wear a swimsuit and nothing else, so he shouldn't polish his baseball spikes or wash his head sweatband. His forehead should show. Looks count.

Looks were even more important for Eugene. Over at his house this morning he brushed his black hair until it stood up in a thick bramble. He fierced his face into a couple of new scowls. He rehearsed his welcoming speech for the Mr. Arlington contest.

"Welcome, Turkey," he growled.

He used his sweetest growl. He unballed his fists. He wouldn't be needing them today. Randy had convinced him to be nice to Zan and Rinehart; otherwise they might cancel their Spectacular.

Not to cancel! Eugene aimed to win it. He'd rot first before he'd lose to Randy Boyle again. Mightiest or not, Randy couldn't be everything—everybody— in fifth grade: Star Athlete, Hit Man, Captain, and now maybe Mr. Arlington. Eugene planned to lift better than Randy, whatever lifting meant. It probably had something to do with welcoming. Zan had put Eugene in charge of that, so it must be important. He would say "Hi, guys" to every meathead in the wrecky garage.

Eugene hated that garage. He was going there at 6:00 p.m. Darn. He didn't want to get his new swimsuit filthy. Would the contest include lifting piles of dirt? Rinehart must be slouchier than ever to hold his contest near those creamed flowers.

"They stink," Eugene said in the tone he planned to use welcoming.

Meanwhile, the garage was also getting ready to

welcome Eugene and the other sports stars. Morning sun streamed through the open windows. Puffs of spring air fanned the giant ferns. Their pots now stood on a platform made out of shelves taken down and hammered together. Nearby, on the same platform, Rinehart's weights waited to be lifted. Someone had painted them golden yellow. They caught the light and sparkled. The stage was set.

In the house Rinehart ate breakfast. He cleaned up a plate of cupcakes Zan made for their team party yesterday. Together they'd celebrated his final lift, press, raise, squat, curl, fly, snatch, chin-up, pull-down, row, and jerk. He'd finished Buster's last chapter.

Rinehart knew precisely what to do at a lifting contest. And what not to do.

One thing Rinehart should do before Zan phoned: that was take chairs to the gym. He stacked four on his shoulder. He opened the back door. With ease Rinehart carried his stack along the driveway. On a day like this he could keep walking to China and not count his steps.

Zan phoned Rinehart on the dot of 10:00 a.m. She'd been thinking. She was full of help for their Lifting Spectacular.

"Wear your disguise," she said.

Rinehart agreed.

"Please don't eat much today. You'll want to lift quick, not just heavy."

Rinehart said, "Yes."

"You'll want to save room for refreshments. Fritz is bringing them, remember?"

Rinehart remembered.

"I've memorized my announcements," Zan said.

"That's lovely."

"Are you set to crush the other lifters?" Zan wanted to be sure.

Rinehart nodded. Zan couldn't see whether the answer was yes or no. She cheered "Gimme an S-T-A-R" on the phone to her favorite athlete and hung up.

Zan went to her room and ironed her announcer's uniform for the third time this Saturday morning. The bow tie smelled scorched. Her jeans could stand up by themselves, she'd sprayed so much starch on them. She dusted her sneakers with baby powder. She'd surprise Rinehart with how good she looked.

And he'd surprise Zan with the swimsuit he'd made. She knew about it, but hadn't seen the color. He'd used yellow paint they found on a garage shelf. Rinehart's lifting uniform would match the weights Zan painted.

The Hit Man's lifting uniform wouldn't match anything. Randy would be wearing himself.

Today at noon Randy gazed into his mother's full-length mirror. What a knockout! The best-looking guy in his school. No need to shine up the zipper on his red-white-and-blue jacket. He'd shine up himself.

All over his body Randy rubbed baby oil. He squished it out of a plastic bottle. He rubbed his arms and legs, wishing he could be Mr. Arlington in June, not this evening in April. By June he would have a tan from baseball season. His tan would glisten under baby oil. He studied his pale color a long time in the mirror. No problem—his freckles glistened.

"But I'm not just another pretty face," he said to his face. "I'm the best athlete in my school. I'll lift anything those creeps tell me to. I'm winning."

He decided to donate his winning shirt to Fritz. Fritz might as well be RANDY when Randy changed his name to Mr. Arlington. Randy gave himself a loud whistle in the mirror and answered the ringing phone.

All afternoon Fritz kept calling. First his swimsuit wouldn't fit right. He didn't have a thing to wear, he complained to Randy.

"Wear baby oil," Randy advised.

Second, Fritz asked his captain how to cook refreshments.

"Bring a knuckle sandwich. Or make your sister cook cookies—around a thousand of them for each lifter and extra ones for the winner. Me."

The next time Fritz phoned, Randy's line was busy. He was talking to DumDum. They talked about keeping score. DumDum said his fingers felt tired already from all the counting he would have to do on them as official scorekeeper. He wanted to hang up and rest them before he won Mr. Arlington.

Randy said, "DumDum—you dodo—I'm winning."

Randy slammed the phone down, but it rang again. This time Eugene wanted to try out his bullet stare he planned to use on the audience when he won Mr. Arlington.

"Genie—you won't win," Randy predicted. "I'm Mr. Arlington already."

The four teammates continued quarreling on the phone until they swore they wouldn't go to the contest at all. No. Never! They wouldn't walk together to 1714 Glebe Road today or any day. No way! It didn't matter to them that Fritz had spent hours in the hot kitchen making cream puffs from a secret recipe his sister let him have.

"You eat 'em. I'm not going," Randy yelled on the phone.

And if Randy wasn't going to the Mr. Arlington Lifting Spectacular, no one was going. Take it from them!

DumDum got there first. He gave Rinehart's garage the once-over. It wasn't all that shabby. He sat down in a front-row chair and propped his feet on the roomy stage. Yep—he felt winnerish. He wouldn't miss Fritz's goodies. He also planned to eat the little flowers growing low under these bushy green trees in front of him. They might taste as good as the leaves he ate last time he came over to Rinehart's.

"Hello, Walter. Welcome, Eugene." Rinehart arrived right before Eugene. He congratulated both lifters on their perfect uniforms. He offered them a glass of lemonade from a bucket on the workbench. Rinehart said the other refreshments would be there soon with Fritz.

"Fritz won't come. Anyway, we don't need him to play lifting." Eugene retied the string on his swimsuit. He meant business.

Fritz came through the garage door shouting to his ex-teammates: "ME. ME. ME. I'm your winning lifter, now that Randy isn't coming." He set down his package of cream puffs on the workbench. It felt heavy after his long walk. Randy showed up in another few minutes. He didn't shout. His body said it all. He glowed. His swimsuit was white with blue stars. Those stars seemed to twinkle.

On his bare chest Randy had printed in Magic Marker ink: MR. ARLINGTON.

Mr. Arlington: II 11

Here they are together in Rinehart's gym. All except Zan Hagen, and she arrives in the nick of time to check everything for slouchiness.

The lights are on, the windows open. Six cream puffs sit neatly on the workbench beside a bucket of punch. Four boys sit in a row, waiting to win, waiting to find out what the heck lifting is. Zan admires their swimsuits. She thanks them for coming. Just before she jumps up on stage to announce, she checks out Rinehart.

Poor Rinehart.

He stands near a window wearing his sweet expression and brown-checkered jacket. His brown eyes hide behind the same old glasses. His school pants seem shorter and tighter, but only if you look carefully. From where the other lifters sit he's Turkey Rinehart, same as ever.

Rinehart's disguise is working.

Zan begins to announce: "The Saturday Evening Sports Spectacular." Her voice is low and steady as she reads from the line-up of stars:

EUGENE

FRITZ

WALTER

RANDY

ARTHUR

"Arthur who? Who's this Arthur?"

Rinehart whispers, "Me."

Eugene yells "Welcome" when Zan invites him on stage. "Ahum," he continues. He blinks at the audience. He's all finished welcoming but he stays on stage to be the first lifter. He sheds his warm-up jacket. Zan tells him to pose. She tells DumDum to give Eugene a score for posing.

She says, "Walter, give each poser a grade. Give A or B or C, like our teacher gives in school. You won't have to add up the alphabet."

Eugene demands, "Gimme an A."

"Don't you ever smile?" DumDum asks.

Eugene turns up his lips in an effort to win posing.

"Not to notice," DumDum insists. "Eugene, you get C. Smiling counts."

Eugene's eyes narrow in fierce slits. Before he can kill the scorekeeper, Zan announces: "And now, Eugene, for the lifting part of this Sports Spectacular. You must lift 100 pounds over your head." Zan points to the barbell with its golden weights attached to each end. They've been sort of hidden under all the ferns lining the stage.

Eugene bends down behind those ferns and tugs at the barbell. Five tugs later he is fuming. He calls the weights "Meatheads." He jerks hard but stands up empty-handed. His mouth hasn't scared the barbell the way it used to scare Zan. Eugene can't frighten iron. His face is blank with shock. He stumbles off-stage and rattles his chair sitting down.

Zan announces: "Eugene *doesn't* lift. Fritz Slappy, you're our next contestant."

Fritz leaves his chair in dread. Shaking, he climbs onstage. How can he pose if Randy doesn't go first to show him exactly what moves to make? How can Fritz ditto what he hasn't seen yet? He glances at the audience, hoping for help from his captain. Fritz seems lost in greenery on stage. He knows he can't pose.

"Pose like this," Rinehart suggests when Randy doesn't volunteer.

"Ha ha ha ha," the audience burst out. They're roaring at poor Rinehart.

He is raising his arms in a V above his head. Boy, does he look silly. His jacket is much too pinchy all over and the collar hikes up to his ears. With a loud ripping sound the jacket sleeves pull out of their sockets.

Fritz is laughing so hard he can't pose. He wipes tears away on a fern so he can find the barbell under-foot.

Walter calls, "F. That's your grade, Fritz. Laughing isn't posing."

Fritz answers by lifting the barbell. He grabs one end with both hands. He lifts that end up to his stomach. The barbell's other end sits still near a fern. Zan has to remind Fritz to pick the barbell completely off the stage floor.

"Show him, Rinehart," the audience hoot together.

Zan announces: "Arthur Rinehart will show you how he lifts when his turn comes. Please, gentlemen, wait for his turn." She quiets the audience by reading the official rules of lifting: " 'The lifter must grip the barbell and pull it in a single movement from the floor to above his head. The bar must pass along the body in a smooth movement.' "

Fritz tries to lift again. "Heave," Randy coaxes him.

"Attaboy, Fritz." Rinehart notices an inch of daylight between the stage floor and the barbell Fritz lifts. "Waytogo," Rinehart cheers for the next inch, the next inch until there isn't any next. Fritz drops the barbell. He topples over backwards. "Nuts to that. You lift this heavy iron, Randy."

Randy leaps onstage. "My turn."

"No, it's Walter's turn," Zan insists.

Randy's eyes prowl the gym. He pretends not to know his friend he nicknamed "DumDum." "Who's Walter?"

"Me. Here I am. Stand back!"

DumDum waits for the stage to clear. He needs space for his pose. He smooths a wrinkle in his swimsuit and steps through the ferns. Posing begins in earnest. Walter wants to prove how tall he is. He doesn't squat or bend. He reaches in only one direction—up. He stands stiff and tall. He makes sure the ferns don't hide his long legs from the row of rowdy boys below him.

"Boo boo, DumDum."

"Aw, fellows, give me a break," Walter pleads.

"Lift the weights," Randy shouts.

"Before that Walter has to award himself a posing score," Zan announces.

Walter doesn't hesitate. He says, "A—my first A ever. I'm the tallest. I can smile all night. I have the least wrinkles."

"How many?" Randy asks.

Zan announces: "Walter is not on stage to count. He's there to lift 100 pounds." She holds up one finger.

"Nothing to it." Walter reaches for the barbell. It comes off the stage floor without a hitch. The bar moves slowly until Walter stands with the golden weights balanced at his waist. He's resting a minute. Sweat breaks out on his forehead.

Rinehart cheers, "YoucandoitWalter."

No, Walter can't do it. He must lift with his brain. His mind must tell his hands to keep on pushing until the bar is high above his head. But DumDum's mind wanders. He's thinking about his A for posing. He's wishing for his sweatband to sop up his forehead. His eyes catch the cream puffs waiting for him on the workbench. Suddenly he thinks, I'm hungry. My arms hurt, my shoulders ache. Aw, I give up. His barbell clangs to the stage floor. Across the gym the lemonade rocks in its bucket.

Rinehart rushes to DumDum's side. He gives him a pat on the back. "Lovely lift," he says. "You've earned an extra cup of lemonade. It matches the color of your wrinkleless trunks."

"Aw, Arthur, lifting hurts bad. Can I have a cream puff?"

"DumDum, you are a cream puff!" Randy snorts in disgust. Not too much disgust, because now Randy knows he's won the contest. His three teammates have bombed. He's the only one left in the garage to become Mr. Arlington.

Randy hasn't noticed that Rinehart has scooped up the barbell and moved it from center stage to clear space for lifting.

Zan announces: "Our Spectacular continues with Randy Boyle."

Everyone claps. Rinehart adds his "Wheeeeo." The audience settle back in their chairs to watch their best-looking-hardest-hitting-star-athlete-captain-number-one-hitter-lifter.

Randy keeps them waiting. He parades around the gym striking poses. He pops a paper cup, swaggers onstage, and pivots. Wow. Randy's dazzling in his red hair, oily muscles, and blue stars. He poses with both hands pointing to his chest.

Walter calls, "A+." He asks Zan, "Can we eat now?"

Zan can't decide. She remembers seeing on TV only the winners eating. To Zan that means all the cream puffs will soon go to Rinehart. But she feels sorry for Walter. He lost the contest. He's hungry, so hungry that he's eating a yellow flower. Zan wonders where he found it. She's too busy watching Randy lift to hunt for blossoms on the stage.

The weights rise swiftly from the floor up to

Randy's stars. From the stars to the Mr. Arlington letters on his chest, the weights rise slowly. Slower from his neck to his chin. At Randy's nose the weights stop. His cheeks fill with air. He lets it out with an "Uffff." His face matches his hair, and it's not a sudden sunburn, either. It's strain. The barbell reaches Randy's eyes with an "AAAARRRRGGGG."

Zan knows the weights won't rise much higher for Randy. His athlete's muscles aren't enough to win at lifting. He needs more, the power that comes from lifting every day on a schedule—hours, months.

Down below Randy, his pals stamp and cheer and slap each other's knee.

"Yep. Yep. Yep."

"See that, Meathead? Randy's winning!"

Rinehart approves with a dozen soft whistles as the weight moves from Randy's eyes to his eyebrows. Oh oh. Randy's eyes say "Help."

Zan wants to help. She's never seen anyone in so much pain, not even Rinehart on his hardest days of lifting. She steps toward Randy, but before she can reach him—

Kaboom. Randy crumples under the strain. The barbell lands near ferns. Pots scatter, and for a change the boys struggle to save them. They can't lift weights but they sure can catch pots. Not one plant hits the cement floor.

In the confusion Rinehart and Randy work side by side lining the pots straight. It takes Rinehart a jiffy to lift them, Randy notices. That makes him edgy. He says, "Seeing as how the contest is over, I guess we can drink up." He pours paper cups full of lemonade. He serves them. The boys mingle and whisper.

85

They forget they can't lift. The Saturday Evening Sports Spectacular is over.

Not quite.

Zan announces: "Rinehart lifts now."

Her voice is soft and pleasant. What can the other athletes do except sit back down to watch? They wink at each other.

Onstage Rinehart undresses. Zan holds his torn jacket, his shirt, his undershirt—

"*Wow,*" Fritz admits. He sees Rinehart's naked chest. No wonder his jacket was popping its checkers. And Rinehart's arms. Where did those come from? Not a sleeve in the gym would fit Rinehart.

Walter calls, "Look what's under his glasses. Real eyes."

Rinehart freezes in a graceful pose.

He holds it long enough for the audience to see his wide shoulders, deeply muscled chest, and hard, flat stomach. He raises his arms. He tenses. From his fingertips to his shouldertops his arms are one long muscle.

Eugene's fuming again. "He makes us guys look like turkeys."

Rinehart relaxes. He drops drown on one knee. Only his head and neck show above the ferns. He's smiling wider than when the Hit Man used to give him twenty-five pennies. Rinehart's face muscles draw his lips up higher and higher.

Walter's wondering, What're those braces on his teeth? His muscles could hold every tooth up.

In pose after pose Rinehart shows his Mr. Arlington body. Bap. Bap. Bap. Bap. Stand up. Left turn.

Half turn. Tense the thighs. Flex the calves. Hands on hips. Strike a front pose, side pose, squatting pose. Move from one to the other smoothly. Never the same pose twice. Rinehart is enjoying himself.

Fritz is thinking, Gardening must be good for muscles.

Another quick turn and Rinehart shows his back It's broad. There're muscles on top of muscles. They begin at his shoulders and don't disappear until the top of Rinehart's trunks covers them with flowers.

Zan loves Rinehart's new swimsuit. He must have made it from cut-off school pants. He's painted yellow flowers all over it. She watches those flowers move around the stage. They're bright and fresh. They seem to be growing now on this fern, now on that fern, spreading toward Rinehart's posing muscles.

Zan looks closely at those ferns. She looks and looks. She sees real flowers growing in those pots. She can't drag her eyes from them. Oh, lovely.

Rinehart's ferns have live flowers! Delicate little red ones, blue ones, yellow ones! Zan checks from pot to pot. The violets, the begonias, impatiens—all the wrecked flowers she planted around the ferns are blooming. The blooms twine among Rinehart's favorites. They've all grown together.

"Arthur, I kept my promise twice," Zan tries to tell him over the screaming audience. "Your ferns have flowers."

Her ears fill up with claps and noisy whistles. Zan hears Fritz announce, "The Lifting Champion of Arlington County, ladies and gentlemen, Mr. Arthur Rinehart." She is holding so many blossoms she can't shake hands with the losers.

She hears Randy say "Ditto."

Zan finally looks up from the flowers to see Eugene smiling and Walter eating cream puffs with both hands. "I missed seeing Rinehart lift," she confesses. "I was watching our ferns bloom."

"See me now," suggests her best friend. He has a scheme, an ending of his own.

Rinehart doesn't bend to pick up his barbell. He doesn't hoist a fern pot. Instead, he catches Walter in a soft hug. He lifts him onto the stage. He lifts Eugene and sets him down near Walter. He lifts Fritz next. He lifts Randy beside Fritz. The boys stand together in a friendly pose. They crunch cream puffs.

Then Rinehart lifts Zan.